JESS JOINS FRIENDS AND FAMILY

ENJOY FAMILY
FRIENDS &

Jess Joins Friends and Family

Written and Illustrated by

GEORGIE HERZ

JOR-G PUBLISHING
ST. LOUIS, MISSOURI

JESS JOINS FRIENDS AND FAMILY
© 2018 Georgene Herz

Printed in the United States of America

ISBN: 978-0-692-13017-9

Jor-G Publishing
St. Louis, MO
jessbooksbygeorgie@gmail.com

Ordering Information: Special discounts are available on quantity purchases by schools, childcare providers, and more. For details, contact the author at the address above.

Book design: Cathy Wood
Editor: Donna Brodsky
Consulting: Meghan Pinson

Children's books by Georgie Herz
Jess Likes to Jump
Jess Joins Friends and Family

TO MY GRANDCHILDREN
AND LEFTY, MY DOG, WHO NEVER
LEARNED TO FETCH

When Mom and Dad say,
"Put your screen away."

Jess says, "I'll play with my friends today."

Jan likes to paint
their toenails blue.

Jess wants to have some
pink ones, too.

Jess enjoys making masks
with Larry.

The two work hard to
make them scary.

Jess and Dale think
dressing up's fun.

Queen or king, they each
must pick one.

Terry and Jess act like
heroes strong.

Later, Jess sings the baby a song.

Jess and Lee find shirts
to tie-dye,

then create a bright kite to fly.

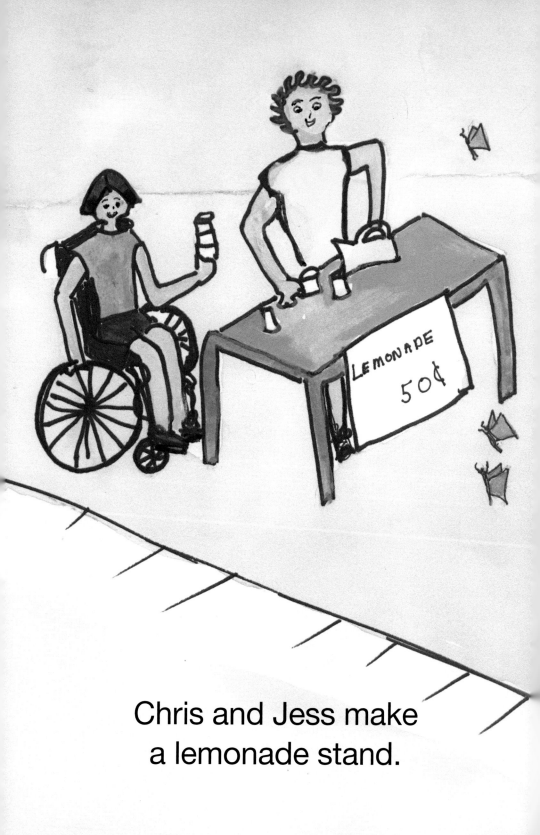

Chris and Jess make
a lemonade stand.

Everyone says the
lemonade's grand.

Swinging is fun with little sis.

They do fancy tricks—just like this.

Stan and Jess throw a ball to Jack.

He catches it, then brings it back.

Dad enjoys teaching Jess to bake.

Mom says to Jess,
"Your cake is great!"

Dad and Jess sew a big
green dragon.

Mom and Jess fix a broken wagon.

"Jess, you've had a busy day,

so now it's time for you to say…
GOOD NIGHT."